A Note to Parents and Caregivers:

*Read-it!* Readers are for children who are just starting on the amazing road to reading. These beautiful books support both the acquisition of reading skills and the love of books.

 The PURPLE LEVEL presents basic topics and objects using high frequency words and simple language patterns.

 The RED LEVEL presents familiar topics using common words and repeating sentence patterns.

 The BLUE LEVEL presents new ideas using a larger vocabulary and varied sentence structure.

 The YELLOW LEVEL presents more challenging ideas, a broad vocabulary, and wide variety in sentence structure.

 The GREEN LEVEL presents more complex ideas, an extended vocabulary range, and expanded language structures.

 The ORANGE LEVEL presents a wide range of ideas and concepts using challenging vocabulary and complex language structures.

When sharing a book with your child, read in short stretches, pausing often to talk about the pictures. Have your child turn the pages and point to the pictures and familiar words. And be sure to reread favorite stories or parts of stories.

There is no right or wrong way to share books with children. Find time to read with your child, and pass on the legacy of literacy.

Adria F. Klein, Ph.D.
Professor Emeritus
California State University
San Bernardino, California

Editor: Jill Kalz
Designer: Joe Anderson
Creative Director: Keith Griffin
Editorial Director: Carol Jones
Managing Editor: Catherine Neitge
The illustrations in this book were created digitally.

Picture Window Books
151 Good Counsel Drive
P.O. Box 669
Mankato, MN 56002-0669
877-845-8392
www.capstonepub.com

Printed in the United States of America in Stevens Point, Wisconsin.
062010
005851R

All books published by Picture Window Books
are manufactured with paper containing at least
10 percent post-consumer waste.

**Library of Congress Cataloging-in-Publication Data**
Jones, Christianne C.
Back to school / by Christianne C. Jones ; illustrated by Ryan Haugen.
p. cm. — (Read-it! readers)
Summary: Jamal, who will be in the fifth grade, and his little sister Anisa, who is
going into first grade, go shopping for school supplies.
ISBN-13: 978-1-4048-1166-9 (hardcover)
ISBN-10: 1-4048-1166-4 (hardcover)
[1. Writing—Materials and instruments—Fiction. 2. Brothers and sisters—Fiction.
3. Shopping—Fiction. 4. African Americans—Fiction.] I. Haugen, Ryan, 1972– ill.
II. Title. III. Series.

PZ7.J6823Bac 2005
[E]—dc22                                                                          2005003738

# School

by Christianne C. Jones
illustrated by Ryan Haugen

Special thanks to our advisers for their expertise:

Adria F. Klein, Ph.D.
Professor Emeritus, California State University
San Bernardino, California

Susan Kesselring, M.A.
Literacy Educator
Rosemount–Apple Valley–Eagan (Minnesota) School District

PICTURE WINDOW BOOKS
Minneapolis, Minnesota

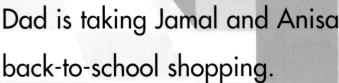

Dad is taking Jamal and Anisa
back-to-school shopping.

Jamal is starting fifth grade.

Anisa is starting first grade.

Jamal needs markers.
Anisa wants some, too.

Anisa gets crayons instead.

Jamal needs a binder.

Anisa wants one, too.

Anisa gets a folder instead.

Jamal needs blue and black pens.

Anisa wants some, too.

Anisa gets pencils instead.

13

Jamal needs narrow-ruled notebooks. Anisa wants some, too.

Anisa gets wide-ruled notebooks instead.

NOTEBOOKS

COLORED PENCILS

15

Jamal needs a bottle of glue.

Anisa wants one, too.

Anisa gets a glue
stick instead.

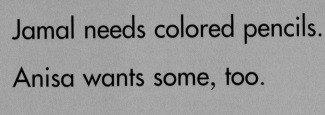

Jamal needs colored pencils.

Anisa wants some, too.

COLORED PENCILS

COLORED PENCILS

Anisa gets watercolors instead.

Jamal needs a book bag.

Anisa needs one, too!

Jamal and Anisa are ready for school.

And Dad is ready for a nap!

# More *Read-it!* Readers

Bright pictures and fun stories help you practice your reading skills. Look for more books at your level.

*Bamboo at Jungle School* by Lucie Papineau
*The Best Snowman* by Margaret Nash
*Bill's Baggy Pants* by Susan Gates
*Camping Trip* by Christianne C. Jones
*Cleo and Leo* by Anne Cassidy
*Fable's Whistle* by Michael Dahl
*Felix on the Move* by Maeve Friel
*I Am in Charge of Me* by Dana Meachen Rau
*Jasper and Jess* by Anne Cassidy
*The Lazy Scarecrow* by Jillian Powell
*Let's Share* by Dana Meachen Rau
*Little Joe's Big Race* by Andy Blackford
*The Little Star* by Deborah Nash
*Meg Takes a Walk* by Susan Blackaby
*The Naughty Puppy* by Jillian Powell
*Selfish Sophie* by Damian Kelleher
*The Tall, Tall Slide* by Michael Dahl

Looking for a specific title or level? A complete list of *Read-it!* Readers is available on our Web site:
**www.picturewindowbooks.com**